Aristotle

JAMESKi'14

WEIRD-Os
Cuz We're Not
Perfect Either!

Written by Aristotle

Illustrations by James Kirk

Aristotle, a small ant with licorice legs and candy cane antennae, loved to play the saxophone, eat peanuts, and read stories; he sat on his half-eaten peanut and began to read a story about the town of Sublime, to the children who were lying on a blanket in the middle of a field.

Once upon a time, there was a queen named Little Miss Perfect, and she ruled the land of Sublime. Like all lands, however, Sublime was not perfect. There were fish that lived in nests, dogs that said "meow", trees without leaves, and throughout the land, lived the Weird-Os.

The queen lived in a beautiful castle that was always kept perfect. Every morning, she woke up and waited for her servant Cutie Pie. Cutie Pie worked for the queen and helped her with her day-to-day tasks. Her first task was always to help the queen get dressed. She would enter the great bedroom as the sun rose, warming the land of Sublime. The roosters would crow, the dogs would meow, the smell of fresh bread would fill the air, and the dew would dance to the sky, knowing that it would return again the next day. The queen always had her shoes on, and Cutie Pie would help her pick out the perfect outfit for the day. But today was different: for some reason, Little Miss Perfect had not put on her shoes yet. As Cutie Pie walked in, she noticed something about the queen that was different... Something that was not perfect. Little Miss Perfect had six toes instead of five! Cutie Pie acted as if she had not noticed, and the queen quickly slid on her shoes, thinking Cutie Pie had not seen her six toes!

Cutie Pie helped the queen dress, and just like every other day, the queen left her to clean the room as she walked down to the dining hall. Two other servants, Kizzup and Yezman, greeted their queen as she arrived for breakfast. These two always told Little Miss Perfect the answer they thought she wanted to hear, whether it was right or wrong. The queen liked to have them around her, because they made her feel like everything was perfect. We know, however, that there is no such thing as perfect, and that we should embrace all of the imperfections of other. Everyone is different, and that's what makes us special! If everyone was the same, everyone would be boring. That would be no fun!

Little Miss Perfect ate her delicious breakfast and drank her hot tea. Kizzup told the queen how beautiful she looked, even though she had oatmeal stuck to the side of her mouth. The queen's reply was the question she often asked: "Am I perfect?" Yezman quickly answered, "Yes my queen, you are beautiful and perfect in every way," as he tried not to stare at her oatmeal-covered cheeks.

As the town came alive, the sun smiled upon Sublime, climbing higher in the sky. A Weird-O known as 4-Eyes was strolling through town. He walked on the cobblestone sidewalks and enjoyed a fresh blueberry muffin that was still warm from the oven. He noticed a poster pinned to a large, leafless tree. The poster was addressed to all the townspeople, inviting them to come to the yearly Town Fair. It also asked for participants to compete in the events. The winner of the Town Fair Competition would get a trophy, a new bike, and would get to ask anyone they wanted for the first dance at the Full Moon Dance that followed the awards ceremony. This included Little Miss Perfect; she had always been the one that the winner chose for the dance.

4-Eyes was very excited for the Town Fair Competition! He ran home and decided to make a plan. He knew he had to practice if he wanted to compete. With dedication, he knew he could win. The only problem was that he needed help, so he wrote a letter to his friend, Elephant Ears. He explained that he was going to compete and asked if Elephant Ears would help him train. He rolled up the letter and sent it to his friend by Rapid Rabbit Delivery, the mail service in Sublime. The Rabbits put the mail in their satchel and ran as fast as they could to deliver it. The service was fantastic and could usually have a letter delivered within a few minutes. Ten minutes later, 4-Eyes got a Rapid Rabbit response. It said:

> I will be more than happy to help...
> That's what friends are for!
> We start tomorrow.
> Your friend,
> Elephant Ears

The next morning, 4-Eyes sat at his table and ate a yummy, healthy breakfast. He knew that if he ate the right foods, it would help him become stronger and faster. He ate his warm oatmeal with a drop of honey, a slice of whole grain toast, an apple, and he drank a big glass of juice. Outside, the sun rose, waving to the tired moon who was yawning and on its way to bed. Birds sang, fish picked worms from the ground, and squirrels played tag, chasing each other up, down, and around trees. After breakfast, 4-Eyes cleaned his dishes, made his bed, and brushed his teeth. He loved how the toothpaste tasted and made his mouth feel so clean. He walked outside and saw Elephant Ears waiting for him, right on time!

Over the next few weeks, they trained. Elephant Ears would ride a bike while 4-Eyes ran behind him. Then, they would do pushups, sit-ups, and jumping jacks. After drinking some water (because staying hydrated is so important), Elephant Ears would test 4-Eyes with trivia questions. 4-Eyes studied hard and made sure he knew all of the answers. Next, it was off to swim in the lake. 4-Eyes always made sure that he was being watched by Elephant Ears, because he knew it was never safe to swim without a buddy. Every day ended the same. 4-Eyes practiced his favorite event: archery. He would practice aiming his curvy bow and shooting a feathery arrow at the target. Minutes became hours, hours became days, and days became weeks, until at last, after six weeks, training was over. It was a good thing too; the contest was only a day away! 4-Eyes thanked Elephant Ears for all of his help and went to bed early, so he could get lots of rest. He drifted off into dreamland and had a great big smile on his face, as a tiny ant played the saxophone while sitting on a half-eaten peanut in the corner of his room.

T he next day the fairgrounds were alive with action. The smell of popcorn, fried dough, and hot dogs filled the air. Families walked around licking ice cream, played carnival games, and rode the amazing rides. There were smiles everywhere, and everybody seemed to be having a good time. The Town Fair Competition was well on its way, and only a few contestants remained. One of them was 4-Eyes, who had just won the foot race up the hill, around the barn, and back. Elephant Ears had been waiting for him at the finish line, congratulating him and giving him encouragement for the next event.

Little Miss Perfect walked around the fairgrounds with Kizzup on one side of her and Yezman on the other. Cutie Pie walked behind her holding up her long dress so it would not drag in the mud. Little Miss Perfect smiled as both Kizzup and Yezman showered her with compliments. They all walked over to a field with two big circular targets that were filled with hay. The targets had red, white, and yellow circles painted on them with a small black dot directly in the center of the target, known as a 'bullseye.' The targets were for the archery competition, the final event in the contest. Little Miss Perfect sat in her beautiful chair, and Yezman and Kizzup naturally sat on either side of her. Cutie Pie quietly listened and watched, as an announcement echoed over the fairgrounds. It said that only two contestants remained in the competition, and that their scores were a "perfect" tie! The word "perfect" was all the queen heard, and she smiled even more as she let out a long breath. In her head, she thought about how wonderful she was. The announcer explained that this was the final event, and the winner would be this year's Town Fair Champion. He then announced the two contestants' names: Johnny Fairguy and 4-Eyes. Everyone clapped as they entered the field holding their bows. 4-Eyes looked around, but stopped when he noticed Cutie Pie. She stared back, smiled, and waved. 4-Eyes felt funny inside as his heart beat faster. He smiled back and prepared himself to shoot his arrow... But Johnny had the first shot.

Johnny Fairguy removed a long brown arrow with green feathers from his quiver and fired it at the target. The crowd cheered as it hit the target's bullseye. He smiled and waved at the crowd, and he stepped to the side as 4-Eyes stepped up for his turn. The crowd simmered down for a moment as he removed a brown arrow with red feathers from his quiver. He took careful aim and fired. SMACK! The arrow sunk into the bullseye of the second target. The crowd cheered; Little Miss Perfect clapped as well. She was just going through the motions while really thinking to herself, "How wonderful I am to have this tournament for the townspeople!" She was always thinking of herself, never others. Johnny Fairguy shot his second shot and WHOOMPH! It landed in the bullseye. Then 4-Eyes did the same. Johnny fired his third and final shot. THUMP! It once again landed in the bullseye. Johnny had a perfect score! 4-Eyes needed another bullseye in order to tie Johnny.

4-Eyes took position and drew his bow as the crowd went silent. He paused, and then lowered his bow. Whispers filled the crowd; they were a bit confused. He decided to do something crazy because win or lose, what matters is that he gave it his best. He turned and walked another 50 yards back from his target. The crowd's whispering turned to a deafening cheer, as he turned and took aim at the target that now, from so far away, looked half the size.

4-Eyes notched his bow with another red-feathered arrow and drew. The crowd once again went silent. Cutie Pie crossed her fingers behind her back, and 4-Eyes slowly took a deep breath as he released the arrow. The only sound was the arrow slicing through air, searching for its target. THUMP!!!!! It slammed into the bullseye. The crowd exploded with cheers! Cutie Pie jumped up and down happily as 4-Eyes smiled with pride. Even Johnny Fairguy joined in and clapped, acknowledging that 4-Eyes had won. Little Miss Perfect stood and clapped, but thought to herself, "Oh no! Now I have to dance the first dance with that little Weird-O!" After receiving his trophy, 4-Eyes was asked how he managed to hit such an incredible shot from so far away. He responded, "Four eyes are better than two!" Once again the crowd cheered.

Later that evening, the first dance was about to begin, so it was time for 4–Eyes to choose his dance partner. In the spotlight next to the dance floor, Little Miss Perfect stood in her beautiful, flowing gown. Cutie Pie held up the dress's train. As 4-Eyes approached, Little Miss Perfect thought to herself, "Let's get this over with." But then something strange happened, something that had never happened before. 4-Eyes walked right past Little Miss Perfect and extended his hand to Cutie Pie! He asked politely if she would honor him with the first dance. Smiling shyly, Cutie Pie nodded, taking his hand. The lights dimmed and the music began. 4-Eyes and Cutie Pie danced, gazing into each other's eyes. It was if they were the only ones in the room. The townspeople watched with delight, all except Little Miss Perfect. Completely forgetting that she had not wanted to dance with 4-Eyes in the first place, the queen was furious! The more they danced, the angrier she became that someone was picked instead of her. The only ones that noticed her storming off to leave were Kizzaz and Yezman, who ran to catch up with her.

eanwhile, 4-Eyes didn't dance with Cutie Pie once. He didn't dance with her twice. He danced with her until his feet hurt, his legs ached, the music stopped, and the ball ended!

All the while, in her tidy chambers, Little Miss Perfect stomped her feet and clenched her fists. She also screamed an awful lot!

Kizzup whispered to Yezman, "I think someone needs a time out." But he did not dare say it loud enough that the queen would hear.

Little Miss Perfect could not understand why 4-Eyes chose to dance with Cutie Pie over her. "How could that little Weird-O not choose to dance with ME?" she shouted.

"They must be jealous of me," she said at last. "That's it! The Weird-Os are jealous because I'm perfect, and they're not."

Little Miss Perfect was so jealous that she decided that she would make a new rule. Everything in Sublime that was different and NOT perfect would have to go, starting with the Weird-Os. The plan was to round up all of the Weird-Os and put them on a ship that would take them away, never to return. "Yes!" Kizzup agreed. Yezman shouted out, "Of course, right away!" The moon was shining brightly and listening to the conversation, it frowned, knowing that the town would be boring if everything was "perfect" and nobody was different.

Back at the dance, 4-Eyes was helping to clean up after the party had ended. He always liked to help out. He was sweeping up some cookie crumbs, when suddenly, Elephant Ears rushed into the room.

Elephant Ears explained to 4-Eyes what the queen had planned.

4-Eyes's four eyes grew wider and wider, and he asked if Elephant Ears was certain. Elephant Ears explained that he had overheard Little Miss Perfect with his great, big, beautiful ears.

"We have to help Cutie Pie!" shouted 4-Eyes. She had already left the dance.

Inside of the castle, Cutie Pie entered the queen's chambers. She was still smiling from dancing with 4-Eyes!

Little Miss Perfect combed her flowing hair.

"My Queen," said Cutie Pie, "may I help you with that?"

"No you may not," hissed Kizzup, but the queen waved a hand at him.

"Of course she can," said Little Miss Perfect, holding a comb out to Cutie Pie.

Cutie Pie smiled and began to smooth the queen's long hair.

"So," said the queen, "what do you think of my hair?"

"It is lovely," answered Cutie Pie.

"Now tell me," snapped the queen grabbing Cutie Pie by her ropey arms, "what you really think!"

"Oh my!" cried Cutie Pie. "What's wrong?"

"You are jealous of my hair, aren't you?" snapped the queen. "You and those other Weird-Os don't like me, because I am perfect."

"No," sighed Cutie Pie. "We Weird-Os like everyone."

Little Miss Perfect stood up and smiled mischievously. "I don't believe you," she said. "Why else would 4-Eyes want to dance with you, when he could have danced with me?" She ordered Kizzup and Yezman to take Cutie Pie away. A huge tear drop fell from Cutie Pie's single eye as Kizzup and Yezman carried her off to the castle's shadowy dungeon.

Elephant Ears and 4-Eyes approached the castle and watched as Kizzup and Yezman locked Cutie Pie up in a cell. 4-Eyes watched from a distance with his four big eyes as Kizzup pressed down on the 5 little numbers that were the combination for the big, silver lock: 1-2-3-4-5.

A gentle breeze flew in from outside and hugged Cutie Pie. With the breeze came a paper airplane. Cutie Pie unfolded it, and saw that written on the inside of the plane was a note from 4-Eyes, telling Cutie Pie that she would be rescued before morning.

The moon looked down over Sublime as Cutie Pie waited for her rescuers. Just as promised, 4-Eyes and Elephant Ears showed up and pressed 1-2-3-4-5 on the big silver lock. The lock popped, and the creaky door to the dungeon swung open. It was so dark inside that Elephant Ears almost tripped on his own feet.

"Yikes!" he said. "I can't see a thing!"

"Don't worry, my friend," said 4-Eyes. "Just hold my hand. I can see everything."

And he could, thanks to his four, wonderful eyes. The room smelled like old mushrooms and damp feet, and he could see a figure sitting on a very uncomfortable-looking cot.

"Hello there," he whispered.

Cutie Pie turned and tried to look at him, but it was too dark for her to see. Luckily, she recognized the voice. She jumped up and ran through the darkness to the shadowy figures near the doorway.

"Oh 4-Eyes!" cried Cutie Pie, hugging the shape she thought was her beloved dancing partner; only it was so dark, that instead of hugging 4-Eyes, she accidentally hugged Elephant Ears! Even so, she was happy to see both of them, and all that mattered was escaping the dungeon.

"Hold my hand, and we'll get out of here!" whispered 4-Eyes, and in no time, he had led them out of the dark, damp dungeon to the fresh night air.

"Oh thank you, thank you, and thank you!" exclaimed Cutie Pie. This time, she hugged 4-Eyes! In fact, she did more than that…she gave him a kiss on the cheek!

4-Eyes turned bright red, and his mouth twitched like a cat's whiskers.

He tried to say something nice, but all that came out was, "I… er… well… that is… er…"

'I think he's trying to say that he missed you," said Elephant Ears.

"Yes," said 4-Eyes. "That is just what I wanted to say."

The three Weird-Os quietly left the dungeon and ran to the edge of the woods, where a tall lookout tower climbed towards the sky.

In the tower, they discussed what they could do. They had almost decided to leave and build a cabin in the woods where they could hide, but Cutie Pie reminded them that there were other Weird-Os that would need help. Both 4-Eyes and Elephant Ears agreed.

From the lookout tower, Elephant Ears stood, listened, and heard the details of the queen's plan; Little Miss Perfect would put all of the Weird-Os on a boat and ship them away. The three Weird-Os made their own plan. They watched as the sun rose once again, warming the land of Sublime, as the dew danced up to the sky. A rooster crowed, and the smell of fresh baked bread at the baker's shop filled the air.

By the time the sun had completely risen, the queen's guards were already gathering up all of the Weird-Os and bringing them down to the salty docks. Cutie Pie looked sad. She walked to the window and looked out at the castle and the village below. She didn't want to leave Sublime. "I hope our plan works," she whispered. "This is our home."

Just then, they heard noise from down below, in the base of the tower. They heard the creak of a door opening, followed by voices.

"What was that?" asked Cutie Pie. Her friends silently shrugged their shoulders.

The voices got closer and closer. The Weird-Os shivered as the footsteps grew louder and louder.

"I saw them come in here," said one of the voices.

"They must be trying to hide," said another.

Suddenly, the door handle shook and slowly turned. The door swung open. Kizzup and Yezman stood in the doorway, staring directly at the Weird-Os.

"There they are!" exclaimed Kizzup. "I told you they were in here."

"Come with us, Weird-Os," said Yezman.

Yezman reached out to grab Cutie Pie, but 4-Eyes pulled her back with him.

"Quickly!" shouted Elephant Ears as he moved in front of the open window. "Grab my hands!"

"You are trapped with nowhere to run. You must come with us," said Yezman. "There's no escape!"

"Oh yes there is!" yelled Elephant Ears triumphantly, as he pulled 4-Eyes and Cutie Pie right out of the window.

"Oh no!" cried Kizzup. "I wanted to catch them, but I didn't want them to get hurt."

"We were just doing what the queen told us to," said Yezman sadly, as he moved to the window.

The three Weird-Os hurtled towards the ground. The wind blew all around them trying to catch them. The walls of the tower raced by them. 4-Eyes closed all four of his eyes.

S uddenly, they stopped falling.
  When 4-Eyes opened his eyes, he saw a wonderful thing. Elephant Ears had stretched his ears as far as he could, and now they were flying!

"I really love your wings…er…I mean ears," said Cutie Pie.

I kind of like them too," smiled Elephant Ears.

Kizzup and Yezman stared out of the window with their mouths wide open.

"What amazing ears!" said Kizzup.

"Yes, "said Yezman. "I wish I had ears like that."

The three Weird-Os floated up over the trees and disappeared into the clouds.

Later than morning, Kizzup and Yezman led the queen's guards throughout the kingdom of Sublime. Everywhere that a Weird-O went, the queen's men went as well. When they found a Weird-O, they asked them to come along, so the Weird-Os did. The guards did not want to leave a single Weird-O in the kingdom!

Finally, as the afternoon sun climbed higher and higher in the sky, Kizzup and Yezman led a great parade of the queen's men and the band of Weird-Os they had captured. They marched them up and down the streets of Sublime. Some of the Weird-Os were having fun. Some were nervous. Some of the Weird-Os were curious. A few felt like crying.

Just then, a very tiny Weird-O touched Kizzup on the shoulder.

"Yes?" asked Kizzup.

"I'm sorry, sir," said the little Weird-O, "but I have to go to the bathroom. How long is it until we get to where we're going?"

Kizzup just stared at the adorable, good-hearted Weird-O. Suddenly, Kizzup felt guilty, because he was doing something he knew he should not do. He held the little Weird-O's hand and walked him down to the docks with all the others.

Just then, Little Miss Perfect arrived and stood next to Kizzup and Yezman. She watched as the guards escorted the Weird-Os down the dock towards the ship. Little Miss Perfect was so pleased with her plan, she did not notice that Cutie Pie, Elephant Ears, and 4-Eyes were not among the Weird-Os being brought to the ship.

"Why are we here?" asked one of the Weird-O's. Yezman patted him on the head and smiled.

"You are here because the queen asked us to bring you here," he said.

"But why'd she ask you to bring us here?" asked another Weird-O.

"Well," said Yezman. "Be patient, and you shall soon see."

"Not soon enough," mumbled Kizzup. He didn't like tricking the Weird-Os. They were nice to him and Yezman. But the queen was in charge, and he had to do what she said. After all, she was the queen.

"I wish she would hurry up," said Yezman, and Kizzup was thinking the same thing. Everyone liked the Weird-Os... everyone except Little Miss Perfect.

Little Miss Perfect walked down to the boat where all the Weird-Os were being held. She smiled at all who surrounded her. She walked through the crowd, carefully trying not to touch them. She was perfect, after all, and didn't want to get close to others who were not.

"You are very pretty," said a very young Weird-O. The queen ignored her and kept walking until she reached a small set of steps that led up to a raised podium. She took a deep breath and looked out at the Weird-Os. Yezman bowed his head. Kizzup did the same.

"All of you Weird-Os are here," she began, "because you are not perfect and can never be perfect."

The Weird-Os just smiled.

"It has come to my attention that living in the same kingdom as someone so very perfect like me," she continued, "is just too hard for you all."

One Weird-O shook his head. "It's not hard at all," he said. The other Weird-Os nodded in agreement.

The queen raised her hand to silence them. "I knew you would deny that you have grown jealous of me," she said.

Now the Weird-Os looked at one another, confused. They weren't jealous of anyone. The Weird-Os loved and respected everyone!

"Don't deny it!" she snapped. Calming herself with a deep breath, she said, "I can't really blame you for being jealous though. It must be VERY difficult, seeing as how you are all so imperfect."

"Can we go now?" asked one of the Weird-Os.

"Yes," said the queen. "That's actually a very good idea." She snapped her fingers to Yezman and Kizzup, who then turned to the queen's guards and nodded at them. "All of you will get on the big boat behind me," ordered the queen. "I have told the captain to take you far away from here... a place where you won't have to be jealous of anyone, because you will only be with others who are just like you."

"That doesn't sound like very much fun," said one of the Weirdo-Os.

"Yeah," said another. "That sounds booooring."

"I'm afraid I've already made up my mind," said the queen. "Only perfect people get to live in Sublime." She nodded and the guards began to take the Weird-Os onto the boat.

"We'd like to stay," pleaded one Weird-O.

"Please don't make us leave," begged another.

The queen just stood and watched.

"I'm sorry, little buddy,' said one of the guards as he put a Weird-O onto the boat. "But we have to do what the queen tells us too."

Just then, the queen squinted her eyes. She looked one way, then the other. "I don't understand," she said.

"Uh-oh," said Kizzup.

"Uh-oh," agreed Yezman.

"Where are Cutie Pie and her two friends?" She looked at Kizzup.

"Well," said Kizzup. "After they flew off, we went to find them, but we just couldn't."

"We looked everywhere," said Kizzup.

"Well then," replied the queen, "if you were perfect, you could have found them. That means that neither of you are perfect enough to stay in Sublime. I want both of you to get on that boat and sail away with the other Weird-Os."

Kizzup looked at the queen. Then he looked back at the Weird-Os, then back at the queen again. He smiled. "I think I would rather go with the Weird-Os than stay here," he said.

The guards gasped.

"Me too," said Yezman, and they both got on the boat.

The queen laughed and shook her head. "Guards!" she exclaimed. "Find me Cutie Pie and her friends, or you'll sail away as well!"

All of a sudden, a shadow raced over the docks. Everyone looked up into the sky. Circling the dock was a flying blue Weird-O, holding onto two others.

"You won't have to look very far," said 4-Eyes, as he jumped away from Elephant Ears, grabbing hold of one of the ropes hanging from the boat's mast.

"GET THEM!" screamed the queen.

But now, Elephant Ears and Cutie Pie swooped back up, and 4-Eyes swung down, closer and closer to the queen!

"Look out below!" he cried, but the queen did not react quickly enough. 4-Eyes came swinging down onto her. She fell backwards and tripped over her own feet. Spinning in a circle, she fell over the side of the dock and into the sparkling blue water.

Elephant Ears and Cutie Pie landed next to 4-Eyes. "Do we know how to make an entrance or what?" he laughed.

"Help!" Little Miss Perfect screamed. "I can't swim!"

"She can't swim?" said one of the Weird-O's. "I thought she was perfect."

"Uh -oh," said Elephant Ears.

"We must help her," said Cutie Pie.

"Yes, we must," said 4-Eyes.

The queen splashed in the ocean, waving her hands in the air and gulping up big mouthfuls of water.

4-Eyes jumped up onto the boat. He grabbed a rope hanging from a hook and wrapped it through the hole in his middle. Then he threw the other end of the rope to Cutie Pie. "Hold on tight," he shouted.

"You bet I will!" Cutie Pie replied.

"Wait!" said Elephant Ears. "What should I do?"

"You get some warm towels," said 4-Eyes, as he jumped into the ocean.

The queen was twirling around. Foam and bubbles surrounded her. "Please help!" she screamed again.

"I'm right here," said 4-Eyes. "Grab onto me."

The queen grabbed 4-Eyes by the arms. She stopped splashing. "Ok," said 4-Eyes. "Reel us in."

Cutie Pie pulled on the rope again and again. At last, the queen and 4-Eyes came to the side of the dock. The other Weird-Os gathered around and helped them climb out of the water. Elephant Ears wrapped them both in warm, fresh towels.

"Th-th-th-th-th-thank you," shivered the queen.

"No problem," said 4-Eyes. "I didn't mean to knock you in the water."

"Hip-hip-hooray for 4-Eyes!" cried Elephant Ears.

"HURRAY!" roared everyone else.

"Hey," said a young Weird-O. "Look at the queen's foot. Isn't it neat?" Everyone looked at the queen's foot sticking out from underneath the wet towel. Her shoe had come off in the water, and now her wiggling toes were plain to see...all six of them!

"She has six toes!" said Kizzup.

"Yes she does," said Yezmen.

"Oh no!" cried the queen, and she pulled her foot back inside the towel.

"Why didn't you tell us you had six toes?" asked one of the Weird-Os.

"Because it's horrible," sniffled the queen. "Because it's weird!"

She stood up and ran to the end of the dock. She jumped over the side and onto the boat. "I will get on this boat now," she wept. "I know that the people in the kingdom won't want me to be here anymore, now that they know how different I am."

"Wait!" said Kizzup. "Look." He reached on top of his head and pulled off his hair. "I'm completely bald," he said. "I've been wearing this wig for ten years now. I was afraid of what other people would think." He twirled the wig in the air, and threw it as far as he could into the ocean.

"As for me," explained Yezman, "I snore so loud, I have to sleep with earplugs. Otherwise, I keep waking myself up!"

Everyone laughed. Then another person in the crowd mentioned that he had pointy ears. Another said that the fingers on his left hand were much bigger than the ones on his right. Soon it seemed that everyone was talking about how imperfect they were. Nobody seemed embarrassed at all.

'But...but aren't you afraid of what other people will say?" asked the queen.

"No," said 4-Eyes. "None of us care if someone has something bad to say about us. Our friends wouldn't say anything bad, and that's what really matters. If a person doesn't like you because you are different, then that person isn't a friend anyhow."

"Yeah," agreed Elephant Ears. "If I wasn't different, I couldn't do this." He flapped his ears and took off into the air. Soon he was zooming above everyone as they cheered him on.

"You see," continued Cutie Pie, "our differences are what make us special. If everyone was the same, then no one would be interesting."

"But I thought you would all laugh at me," said the queen.

"Look around," answered 4-Eyes. "No one is laughing. We are your friends."

"You truly ARE my friends," said the queen, astounded. "Even though I was going to make you leave the kingdom, you still care about me."

"Friends forgive and forget," said Cutie Pie.

"So you really don't want me to leave?" asked the queen.

"Leave?" said Elephant Ear, as he landed next to the queen. "I want to see that foot of yours. It's BEAUTIFUL!" He helped her step off the boat and back onto the dock.

As the queen stood upon the dock, she paused and thought to herself. "My friends," said the queen finally, "from this moment forward, everyone is welcome in the kingdom of Sublime. It doesn't matter if you have big ears, or four eyes..."

"Or even six toes," said Elephant Ears.

The queen smiled. "Or even six toes," she concluded.

"Hip-hip-hooray for Little Miss Perfect," shouted someone in the crowd.

"Hip-hip-hooray for...the Weird-Os!" said the queen.

"HIP-HIP-HOORAY!" roared the crowd.

For the first time in the queen's life she realized what perfect was. She realized that everyone was perfect just the way they are.

That night, there was a great and wonderful celebration, and everyone danced and sang along as the Weird-Os' favorite song played. "We love all, big or small," sang the Weird-Os,

"CUZ WE'RE NOT PERFECT EITHER!"